BONE
ADVENTURES

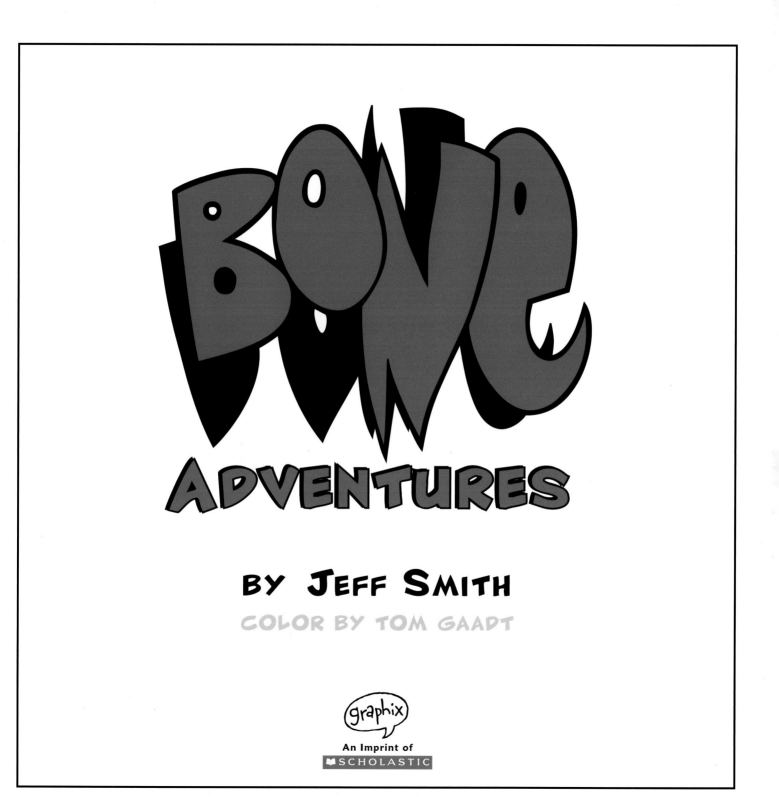

BONE ADVENTURES

BY JEFF SMITH
COLOR BY TOM GAADT

graphix
An Imprint of
SCHOLASTIC

Library of Congress Control Number available

ISBN 978-1-338-62068-9 (HC) / ISBN 978-1-338-62067-2 (PB)
10 9 8 7 6 5 4 3 2 1   20 21 22 23 24

Printed in China   38
First edition, May 2020
Book design by Jeff Smith and Charles Kreloff

FOR VIJAYA

CONTENTS

The End

JEFF SMITH is the *New York Times* bestselling author of the award-winning BONE series, which is published in over 30 countries and is among *Time* magazine's Ten Best Graphic Novels of All Time. BONE was a pioneer in comics publishing for kids when it launched Scholastic's graphic novel imprint, Graphix, in 2005.

Smith's other award-winning and acclaimed comics include *SHAZAM! The Monster Society of Evil*, RASL, *Little Mouse Gets Ready!*, *Rose*, and *Tall Tales*. Smith splits his time between Columbus, Ohio, and Key West, Florida, with his wife and business partner, Vijaya Iyer. He's busy working on his current project, *TUKI: 2 Million BCE*.